Burglar Bill

Janet & Allan Ahlberg

PUFFIN

Burglar Bill lives by himself in a tall house full of
stolen property. Every night he has stolen fish and
chips and a cup of stolen tea for supper. Then he
swings a big stolen sack over his shoulder and goes
off to work, stealing things.

Every morning Burglar Bill comes home from work and has stolen toast and marmalade and a cup of stolen coffee for breakfast. Then he goes upstairs and sleeps all day in a comfortable stolen bed.

One night Burglar Bill is working in a little street behind the police station.

When he comes to the first house he climbs in through the bathroom window and shines his torch around.

'That's a nice toothbrush,' says Burglar Bill. 'I'll have that!' And he puts it into his sack.

When he comes to the second house he climbs in through the kitchen window and shines his torch around.

'That's a nice tin of beans,' says Burglar Bill. 'I'll have that!' And he puts it into his sack.

When he comes to the third house he climbs in through the bedroom window and shines his torch around.

'That's a nice hat and coat and pair of trousers and socks and shoes,' says Burglar Bill. 'I'll have them!' And he puts them into his sack.

Swinton Library and Neighbourhood Hub

Customer ID: *****2796

Items that you have checked out

Title: Burglar Bill
ID: 550528134R
Due: 02 November 2023

Title: I am actually a penguin
ID: 550246667W
Due: 02 November 2023

Title: Missing Richmond
ID: 550628585C
Due: 02 November 2023

Title: Tidy
ID: 550200166G
Due: 02 November 2023

Title: Whatever next!
ID: 5508888166
Due: 02 November 2023

Total items: 5
Checked out: 5
12/10/2023 14:45

Thank you for using Rotherham Libraries
www.rotherham.gov.uk/libraries

When he comes to the sixteenth house, he stops.
There on the front step is a big brown box with
little holes in it.

'That's a nice big brown box with little holes
in it,' says Burglar Bill. 'I'll have that!'

In the distance the town hall clock strikes five.
'Time to stop work,' says Burglar Bill.

He swings the sack over his shoulder, picks up
the box and goes home to have breakfast.

After breakfast Burglar Bill plays with his cat by the fire. Suddenly he hears a noise.

'Sounds like a police car!' says Burglar Bill.

But the noise is coming from the big brown box, and it is getting louder.

'Sounds like TWO police cars!' says Burglar Bill. He creeps up to the box and raises the lid.

'Blow me down,' he says. 'It ain't no police cars, it's a . . .

. . . baby!'

Burglar Bill puts the baby on the table.

'What was you doing in that box, baby?' he says.

But the baby only keeps on crying.

'All alone,' says Burglar Bill. He pats the baby's little hand. 'A orphan!'

But the baby only keeps on crying.

Then Burglar Bill says, 'I know what you want – grub!'

Burglar Bill gives an apple to the baby. But still
the baby cries.

He gives a slice of toast and marmalade to the
baby. But still the baby cries.

He gives a plate of beans and a cup of tea to the
baby. The baby eats the beans, throws the cup of
tea on the floor and starts to laugh.

'That's better,' says Burglar Bill. 'I like a few
beans meself!'

Burglar Bill sits by the fire and wonders what to do. The baby is crying again.

He gives the baby a football to play with. The baby throws the football at the cat and keeps on crying.

He gives the baby a book to look at. The baby bites a hole in the book and keeps on crying.

He sings a song and plays the piano to the baby. The baby cries louder than ever.

He falls off the piano stool and bangs his nose on the floor.

The baby laughs and shouts, 'Again!'

'Again?' says Burglar Bill. He rubs his nose. 'I didn't want to do it the first time!'

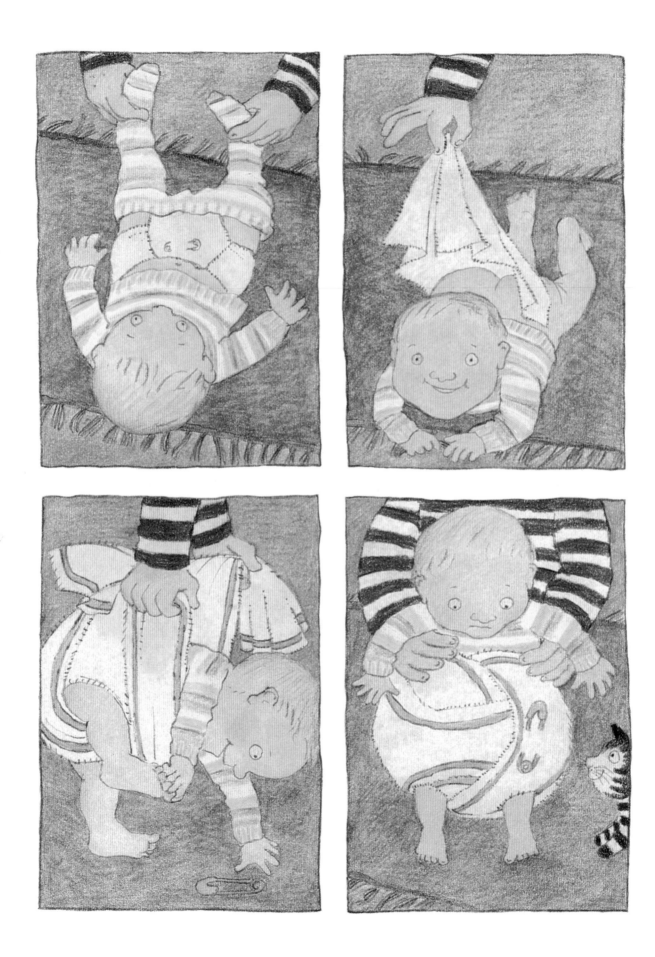

Burglar Bill bounces the baby on his knee.

'So you can talk,' he says. 'Say "Burglar Bill".'

'Boglaboll,' says the baby.

'Say "Peter Piper picked a peck of pickled pepper",' says Burglar Bill.

'Boglaboll,' says the baby.

Suddenly Burglar Bill feels his knee getting wet and smells a smell.

'Poo,' he says. 'I know what YOU want!'

'Poo,' says the baby.

Burglar Bill changes the baby's nappy. He doesn't have another one so he uses an old bath towel instead.

'Say "For he's a jolly good fellow for changing my nappy",' says Burglar Bill.

Burglar Bill plays with the baby and shows it round the house. He feeds it again, changes its nappy again, washes its clothes and hangs them on a line in the kitchen.

When night comes he takes the baby for a walk in
the park.

'Say "Run for it", if you see anybody,' says
Burglar Bill.

'Runfrit,' the baby says.

At twelve o'clock Burglar Bill comes home, puts the baby to bed and goes to bed himself. Soon he is snoring softly and dreaming of his childhood days. Suddenly he wakes up. Downstairs there is a noise.

It is a noise that Burglar Bill has heard before; the noise of someone opening a window and climbing carefully in.

'Blow me down,' says Burglar Bill. 'I'm being burgled!'

Burglar Bill creeps to the top of the stairs.
Down below a torch is shining and a voice says,
'That's a nice umbrella – I'll have that!'
    Burglar Bill creeps down the stairs. The
voice says, 'That's a nice tin of beans – I'll
have that!'

Burglar Bill creeps along the hall and into the
kitchen. The voice says, 'That's a nice date
and walnut cake with buttercream filling and
icing on the top – I'll have that!'
BURGLAR BILL PUTS ON THE LIGHT.

There, with a black mask over her eyes and her hand in the bread-bin, stands a lady.

'Who are you?' says Burglar Bill.

'I'm Burglar Betty,' says the lady.
'Who are you?'

Burglar Bill puts on his own mask.

'Oh,' says Burglar Betty, 'I know you – it's Burglar Bill! I seen your picture in the *Police Gazette*.' Then she says, 'Look here, I'm ever so sorry – breaking in like this. If I'd have known . . .'

'Don't mention it,' says Burglar Bill. He holds out his hand. 'Pleased to meet you.'

'Likewise, I'm sure,' Burglar Betty says.

Burglar Bill makes a jug of cocoa and opens a packet of ginger biscuits. The two burglars sit round the kitchen table.

'You married, Bill?' says Burglar Betty.

'No,' says Burglar Bill. 'The right woman never come along.'

He offers the biscuits to Burglar Betty. She takes one and dips it in her cocoa.

'Only I just wondered,' she says; 'seeing these baby things.'

'Oh, I got a baby,' says Burglar Bill. 'Found it on a doorstep in a box.'

'In a box?' says Burglar Betty.

'That's right,' says Burglar Bill. 'A big brown box with little holes in it.'

'A big BROWN box with little HOLES in it?' says Burglar Betty.

'That's right,' says Burglar Bill.

'Well blow me down,' says Burglar Betty. 'That baby's mine!'

The two burglars hurry upstairs to the baby's room.

'That's him!' says Burglar Betty.

She swings the baby in the air.

'You see, he's got this little birth mark on his leg! And these are his own little clothes as well, what his grandma knit him.'

Back in the kitchen Burglar Bill makes a fresh jug of cocoa and opens a packet of arrowroot biscuits. Meanwhile, Burglar Betty tells him how she lost the baby.

'You see, I just left him on that doorstep for a minute while I was burgling the house, and when I come out he was gone! I thought the police had got him.'

'I only thought it was a useful sort of box,' says

Burglar Bill. 'I never knowed there was a baby in
there till I got it home.'

Burglar Betty gets ready to leave.

'I suppose your husband'll be glad when you get
back,' says Burglar Bill.

'No he won't,' says Burglar Betty. 'I ain't got no
husband.'

She dabs a little hankie to her eyes.

'You see, I'm a widow-lady.'

Burglar Bill walks through the town with
Burglar Betty and the baby.

'You know, Betty,' he says, 'getting
burgled like that give me a fright.'

'I know what you mean,' says Burglar
Betty. 'Losing my baby like that give ME a fright.'

'I can see the error of my ways,' says
Burglar Bill. 'I've been a bad man.'

'Me too,' says Burglar Betty. 'I've been a
bad woman – I've been a TERRIBLE woman!'

Just then the baby starts to cry.

'Sh!' says Burglar Betty. 'You'll have the
police after us.'

Burglar Bill looks over his shoulder.

'From now on I'm going to lead a honest
life,' he says. 'And all them things I've pinched –'

'All them things I'VE pinched as well,' says
Burglar Betty.

'All them things,' says Burglar Bill, 'mine
and yours, Betty, we're going to . . .'

'. . .TAKE THEM BACK!'

WANTED

Burglar
Bill

DESK

PIKE

Red
Cow

So Burglar Bill stops being a burglar and, after a time, starts working as a bread-man in the local bakery. Burglar Betty stops being a burglar as well. When spring comes she sells her house and gives the money to the Police Benevolent Fund. Then she gets married to Burglar Bill.

Outside the church Bill stands with the baby in his arms.

'Say "Bakery Bill",' he says.

'Bakery Bill,' says the baby.

'Say "For he's a jolly good fellow for marrying my mum",' says Bill.

'Say "For she's a jolly good fellow for marrying HIM",' Betty says.

In the distance the town hall clock strikes four. Bill, Betty and the baby leave the church, walk down the little street behind the police station and go home to have their tea.

PUFFIN BOOKS
Published by the Penguin Group:
London, New York, Australia, Canada, India, Ireland, New Zealand and South Africa
Penguin Books Ltd, Registered Offices: 80 Strand, London, WC2R 0RL, England

puffinbooks.com

First published by William Heinemann Ltd 1977
Published by Puffin Books 1999
Reissued 2015
008

Made and printed in China

ISBN: 978–0–140–50301–2